Sarah E. Slater

# Bookmark
# Bear

AUSTIN MACAULEY
P U B L I S H E R S   L T D.

## About the Author

Sarah E Slater was born and bred in the beautiful city of Durham. Married, with three young children her days are spent being a home maker, cook, cleaner and chief bottle washer as well as the odd bit of writing.
Her family is her inspiration, motivation and a revelation.

A CIP catalogue record for this title is available from the British Library.

ISBN 978-1-78612-015-1 (paperback)
ISBN 978-1-78612-016-8 (hardback)
ISBN 978-1-78612-017-5 (eBook)

www.austinmacauley.com

First Published (2017)
Austin Macauley Publishers Ltd.
25 Canada Square
Canary Wharf
London
E14 5LQ

## Dedication

I would like to dedicate this book to Oscar, Samuel and Matilda, who take me on my daily adventures.

# CONTENTS

# THE MARKET

The market stalls of Crimpley looked lonely and sad on this grey rainy day. There were people in suits rushing by, heads down and umbrellas up, not looking across to the stalls, barely looking where they were going. There were people sheltering under the stall canopies, feigning an interest in the produce in order to keep out of the rain, but these were few. There was the occasional genuine buyer but even these were hurrying through their purchases, wanting to get home to the warm and dry. Felix and his mum were in this last group. Felix in particular was dreaming of his warm cosy living room, cartoons on TV and perhaps even a hot chocolate treat. Felix's mum was also dreaming of the warm cosy living room (and maybe even the hot chocolate treat) but a good book instead of the TV. Felix's mum loved to read and that's why they were at Crimpley markets.

Every week Felix was dragged to the markets to hunt through the book stalls to find new reading material. Secretly Felix quite enjoyed this trip and loved to find an exciting new adventure book hidden amongst the endless romance novels but he was cold today and tired and nothing was really jumping out at him. He distractedly discarded book after book of various shades of pastels when suddenly a small, square, dark blue book dropped onto the wet floor. 'You'll have to buy that now dearie, it's soaked,' said the market stall owner.

'But… but… I didn't even…' spluttered Felix looking up, then he caught the old lady's eye and she gave him a wink,

'Trust me dearie, I think you'll like that one.'

Felix thought it looked a little dull if he were honest, but he remembered his mum always saying 'Don't judge a book by its cover' – plus, there was something about the stall owner that compelled him to hold onto the book and to trust her. Felix took his pocket money out and counted out the correct change.

'Keep it safe dearie and remember to feed it,' she said with a chuckle.

What did she mean, "feed it"? He must have misheard and she had said "read it" of course.

Felix and his mum rushed back down the high street, the rain bouncing round them until they reached their little flat. They were drenched when they arrived, Felix's mum made him shower and change so that he didn't catch a cold. He then had his tea and Mum let him watch some TV, so it wasn't until he climbed wearily into bed later that evening that he remembered his book and the strange words the stall owner had said to him. He jumped back out of bed to get the book out of his bag. As he walked across the room he swore he heard a little voice coming from his bag:

'I'm hungry.'

Then a very loud growl.

# THE BEAR

Felix started! What was that? He heard the growl again; this time he realised it sounded more like a tummy rumble than a scary growl. What was it? It couldn't be the book, could it? Gurgle gurgle gurgle, the noise came again, followed by a little voice.

'I'm so hungry,' it complained.

It didn't seem such a frightening voice so Felix started to slowly unzip his bag, still half expecting at any moment some grisly creature to jump out… but nothing happened. Felix took a deep breath and peered carefully into his bag, then exhaled, half disappointed, half relieved – there was nothing in his bag but the book and it couldn't possibly be a book talking could it?

**'I'M HUNGRY.'**

This time there was no mistaking it: the voice had definitely come from the book and it was loud and more than a little cross. Felix snatched the book out of his bag, ran to the bed, threw in onto his duvet then stood over it wondering whether he dared open it. It was then he noticed something sticking out of the book. It was a bookmark, but not the usual coloured paper or leather bookmarks his mum had. This book mark was furry and it looked like, could it be, yes it definitely was, a bear – a bookmark bear!

**'BOO!'** said the bear loudly,

Felix jumped and the bear laughed a hearty laugh.

'Now stop messing around and feed me, I'm starving in here you know, a bear can't live on words alone.'

'Eerm what would you like to eat?' said Felix tentatively, starting to recover a little from his shock. 'Honey?' he speculated.

'Don't be ridiculous,' huffed the Bookmark Bear, 'and before you ask I don't eat marmalade sandwiches either.

Got any steak?'

'No I don't think so, and I don't think Mum would be happy if I gave the steak to you if we did... Beans on toast?'

'Now you're talking,' said the bear. 'Two rounds of toast, plenty of butter and some of those little sausages if you can manage that? Quick about it too before I get really grumpy.'

'Oh okay.' Felix hurried downstairs, wondering how he would explain wanting beans on toast when he should be in bed, but Mum had fallen asleep on the couch with her new book resting on her face. Ten minutes later Felix was back in his room, sat on the bed, with a bear that should just be a bookmark, wolfing down a plate of beans and toast.

'Whafphts yohemr naumhe?' humphed the bear with a mouthful of food.

'Felix,' ventured Felix.

'Felix hmmmm, a Latin name, it means happy, fortunate or lucky, don't you know?' said the bear after he swallowed the last of his meal. 'And you are lucky aren't you Felix? You found me after all,' he said grinning. Felix wasn't quite sure what he thought about the bear grinning; grumping seemed to suit him more!

# A NAME

'What's your name?' Felix asked the bookmark.

'Aaaah there's a question. I've had many names over the years and no real name. I'm the bookmark, but as you're my keeper now, that means you get to name me. Nothing stupid now though, you can't imagine some of the names I've had in the past. No wonder I'm grumpy, especially when I know the meaning of them all. One girl, many moons ago called me "Squidgy-pop", I mean can you imagine, a dignified bear like me called "Squidgy-pop"? I've had "Brody", which is fine but means muddy place or ditch; "Caleb", which means dog; "Huslu", which actually does mean hairy bear, so that's fairly acceptable since I am a hairy bear but probably not great for you human types; "Ruskin", and I don't have a hint of red in my hair; even "Bianca" once – where do I begin with that one? I'm not female and I'm not white. You people have a funny way of naming things. I mean, I once knew a boy called "Cameron" and he didn't have a crooked nose at all, a "Boyd" who had black hair, a "Calvin" who had lots of hair…'

Felix began to think the bear would never stop so interrupted him:

'Well,' he said loudly, 'if you could pick a name what would it be?'

'Frank,' said the bear without hesitation.

'Seriously… Frank?' said Felix.

'Yup, Frank. It suits me, don't you think? And it means "Free one",' said the bear with longing in his voice.

'Well maybe we can come up with a compromise,' said Felix hopefully, thinking "Frank" wouldn't have been his first choice. 'For now I'll call you "Bear".'

'Okay,' said Bear, 'let's go.'

'"Let's go?" Where? It's nearly bedtime – I can't go out now.'

'Not out,' said Bear with a mischievous grin… 'IN!'

# INTO A BOOK

'Into a book, that's what we do,' said Bear. 'Now, pick something simple for your first go. It can get quite tricky until you get used to it, you don't want to land in the middle of space or at the depths of the ocean now, do you? Go look on your shelves. Something with a nice bit of open space should do it. I hear the fairy-tales need some work.'

Felix was confused but more than a little curious and went to look at the books on his shelves.

'Watership Down,' he ventured.

'Aaargh never!' shouted Bear. 'Try again.'

'I have "Three Billy Goats Gruff"? That's a fairy-tale.'

'Oooo yes,' said Bear, 'that will do nicely, the Scribingers have been all over the old stories lately. They think nobody reads anymore but it's not true or it shouldn't be true at least.'

Bear sounded wistful, but then pulling himself together almost shouted, 'Bring it over to me and we'll be off.'

Felix opened the book as Bear said, 'Take my paw.'

Felix had no idea what was about to happen but thought that as it had been rather a strange day so far anyway he may as well go with it. He held on to the bear's tiny (but surprisingly strong) paw and Bear began to read.

"Once upon a time there were three billy goats gruff, Little Billy Goat, Middle sized Billy Goat and Great Big Billy Goat………………."

Felix felt funny: Bear's voice seemed far away as if Felix was trying to listen underwater. Suddenly his stomach turned over, like when you're in the car and go over the top of a hill too fast. He felt as if he was falling but could also feel the steady reassuring paw of Bear in his hand. It seemed to be pulling him back from the fog then… bump… the world came into focus again. To be more accurate, a world came into focus, for Felix was certain this wasn't his world. He also felt a little queasy but wasn't about to admit that!

'Not bad for your first trip, boy,' said Bear with another grin. The beans had definitely done the trick, he wasn't half as grumpy now. 'A lot of kids are sick on their first go.'

'A lot of kids? Are there more kids here, what do you mean?' asked Felix, confused.

'Plenty of time for questions later, follow me,' said Bear, stomping off across the barren field they had landed in.

# THE SCRIBINGERS

'Where are we?' asked Felix.

'In the book of course,' said Bear. 'We're here to see what the Scribingers have been up to this time. Scribingers hide in books, you see, and when they think no one will notice they get up to mischief, telling characters to do things they shouldn't do, changing the story, eating the words.'

'Don't people notice?' asked Felix.

'Sometimes,' said Bear, 'but that's why we're here – to change them back as quickly as possible. Most of the time people think they've misread them or children tell their parents who think they've made it up.'

I can believe that, thought Felix.

'Okay look over there Felix, we can see the three billy goats in the field.'

'There's not much grass left,' said Felix.

'That's right,' said Bear, 'that's why they have to cross the bridge to get to the other side. Don't you remember the story?'

'I've not read fairy stories for a long time,' said Felix sheepishly.

'Very underrated, the fairy stories,' lectured Bear, 'much more to them than meets the eye you know, and always a little bit gruesome which all children still like, surely.

'There goes Little Billy Goat Gruff, he's about to cross the bridge; all seems okay so far.'

 Felix watched as the little goat trip-trapped onto the bridge. Suddenly a gruesome knurly troll jumped up onto the bridge. Felix and the bear were too far away to hear what was said but instead of letting the goat cross the bridge the troll grabbed him, lifted him easily above his head and with a triumphant roar jumped down under the bridge again.

'Oh dear,' said Bear, 'this is worse than I thought,' and to Felix's horror he could then hear a horrible crunching

and slurping sound coming from under the bridge despite the distance!

'Shouldn't we have stopped him?' cried Felix.

'Well we didn't want to get eaten as well,' replied Bear. 'Come on, let's move; we need to alter this before too many children read it.'

'How?' questioned Felix.

'Back to the beginning, of course. Quick, grab my paw again.'

Felix felt the swirling, queasy, pulling feeling again and landed with a bump, albeit a soft one this time, back in his bed.

'Now we know what the Scribingers have been up to we need a plan to stop them.'

'I'm not sure I'm keeping up here,' said Felix.

'Sorry,' said Bear, 'I do forget you are new to this, but we have to move fast. The Scribingers are getting more active since the invention of eBooks: they're worried there'll be nowhere for them to live if printed books don't survive!

'In this book the goats keep telling the troll to wait for the next goat coming along who is bigger, fatter, tastier, etc., until the biggest goat crosses and boots the troll off the bridge, never to be heard of again. It's a lesson in greed if you're that way inclined; if not, then it's just a good old yarn. Scribingers have been in the book and it seems they have persuaded the little billy goat not to tell the troll to wait for his bigger, fatter brother to cross the bridge and whatever they have told him to say has gotten him eaten instead! That just won't do.'

'But what are Scribingers and how did they get into the book and how do you know where they are?' Felix had so many questions he felt he was going to burst.

'We need to get back into that book fast before too much damage is done but I see you do need some explanation,' said Bear patiently. 'So…

'Scribingers are a bit like bookworms, bookworms with a mischievous sense of humour and legs of course and they don't actually look at all like worms, but they do live in books. Most of the time they just eat the odd letter, a little bit of punctuation here and there that people don't notice, but, sometimes, if they find a way into a particularly badly written book they become enlivened from all the food and start to get up to mischief, jumping into books and changing them. As for how I know where to go, the Librarian tells me of course, she knows everything about every book ever written.'

Felix wanted to ask who the "Librarian" was and how she could possibly know that but he could tell Bear was getting impatient so thought he'd leave that till they got back – they were coming back, surely!

'Okay,' said Bear decisively, 'we'll need a spade, some rope, sticky tape and a thesaurus.'

'Oh just let me get them out of my drawer,' said Felix.

'I might be a bear,' said Bear, 'but I recognise sarcasm when I hear it. You find the thesaurus and the tape and I'll get the rest,' he huffed.

Felix crept back down stairs, grabbed the thesaurus off the bookcase in the living room (Mum still snoozing on the couch) and the tape out of a kitchen drawer and hurried back to his room. He was surprised to see Bear sat on the book of fairy stories with a full-size spade and large piece of rope next to him.

'But how?' stammered Felix.

'Simple,' said Bear, 'I read myself into Treasure Island – loads of spades and ropes in there.'

'Ooo that sounds like a good book to try.'

Bear laughed and said, 'One step at a time, lad.'

# BACK IN THE BOOK

Bear began to read again. 'Once upon a time there were three billy goats gruff…'

Whoosh – into the book they fell.

This time they arrived a little earlier and all three goats were eating grass in the field.

'Let's go talk to the goats. We need to make it fast so no readers notice us and we really don't want to encounter a Scribinger if we can help it.'

'Why not?' Felix wanted to ask but Bear was off over the field: for a tiny bear, he could really move. He leapt up onto the little goat's back who started and jumped but then calmed down when he saw it was Bear. Felix caught up panting.

'Listen to me,' Bear urged the goats. 'Scribingers have been in the book and changed your lines; you're going to get eaten.'

'Don't be silly,' bleated the goats and carried on lazily eating the grass.

'Please you have to believe us,' begged Felix.

'The Librarian sent us,' said Bear quietly.

'Ooooh!' bleated the goats in unison. 'In that case what should we do?'

'Well what do you say when you get to the bridge?' said Bear to the little goat.

'I say "Hello Mister Troll I'm a fat tasty goat, please may I pass?"'

'Hmmm,' said Bear, 'it's not even subtle!'

Bear explained to the goats what they should be saying and why. It seemed to be taking forever: the goats, in Felix's opinion, were a little slow on the uptake and Felix was feeling nervous.

He mentioned this to Bear. 'I think the Scribingers might be getting near,' said Bear.

All of a sudden there was a whirling of dust and a chattering shrieking noise. 'Uh oh,' murmured Bear. 'They've

found us.'

'Quick, get digging!' he shouted to Felix and, 'Get to that bridge!' to the goats. 'You say what I told you to the troll and you'll be safe,' he yelled at their retreating backs. 'I'll distract them with some long words.'

The goats were moving quite swiftly now; seemingly, the shrieking noise had spurred them on in a way the urging from Bear and Felix had not.

'The Scribingers are coming, Felix,' shouted Bear, 'you keep digging and they'll head towards the words, they won't be able to resist. I'll keep shouting out long words to confuse them and hopefully they won't notice the goats heading the other way.'

Felix didn't know what Bear meant but he started digging anyway. He drove the spade into the ground but instead of hitting mud it felt like paper… words, letters, commas, abbreviations, etc., came spilling out of the hole.

'It's not mud,' he said.

'Of course not,' replied Bear, 'it's a book!' Bear was still bellowing out words that Felix had never heard before and certainly didn't know the meaning of.

The dust cloud got closer and the shrieking louder.

'It's working!' yelled Bear. 'Keep digging and get the sticky tape ready.'

All of a sudden the dust cloud and the shrieking stopped: the silence that followed was almost as deafening. As the dust settled Felix saw the Scribingers. There were only two of them. They were wiry and small and their skin looked too tight; their faces appeared to mainly be teeth. They were a little like the pictures of elves you see in books, the way raisins are little like grapes.

'Fractious… erudite… nadir… inveterate… obsequious…' roared Bear. The Scribingers were heading for the words. 'Now push them in the hole, Felix,' charged Bear.

Felix shoved with all his might, not really wanting to touch the creatures but fearing Bear more, the way he looked at the minute. He suddenly seemed ten times bigger and to radiate an urgency that had to be obeyed.

The Scribingers grabbed at Felix as they fell but he felt a steadying rope round his waist hauling him back away from the hole. The Scribingers grabbed at words as they fell, stuffing them greedily into their mouths.

'Quick,' said Bear, 'tape up the hole.'

Felix quickly found the end of the tape (his mum had folded it over) and sealed the hole in the book/field – Felix wasn't sure which, really.

'Good job Felix, now let's get out of here.'

As Felix took Bear's paw he looked over towards the bridge just in time to see the great big goat kick the troll over the side. Then they were swirling back to his room. It felt a little like flying now he was getting more used to it, and the landing back in his room was a soft one.

# HOME

'Wow,' said Felix, 'WHAT HAPPENED?'

'You saved the book,' said Bear, grinning. 'The Scribingers will be lost for a while between pages. They'll be back but we'll let the Librarian worry about that. For now you need to get some rest.'

'There's so much I want to ask though and I couldn't possibly sleep.'

But even as he said this his eyes were feeling itchy and heavy. He crawled into bed and pulled the covers up; as he was drifting away, he muttered sleepily, 'Who is the Librarian?' and he heard a faint growly chuckle say: 'That's for another story.'

A short while later Felix's mum crept into his room to check he was asleep. Crossing to the bed she saw that Felix, who was sleeping soundly, had two books gripped tightly to his chest: one was open at a page with sticky tape across it; the other had a furry bookmark in it that looked like a bear.

It was probably a trick of the light, but as she turned to leave the room, the bear winked at her! Felix's mum just smiled.

## THE END